The Moccasin Goalie

ORCA BOOK PUBLISHERS

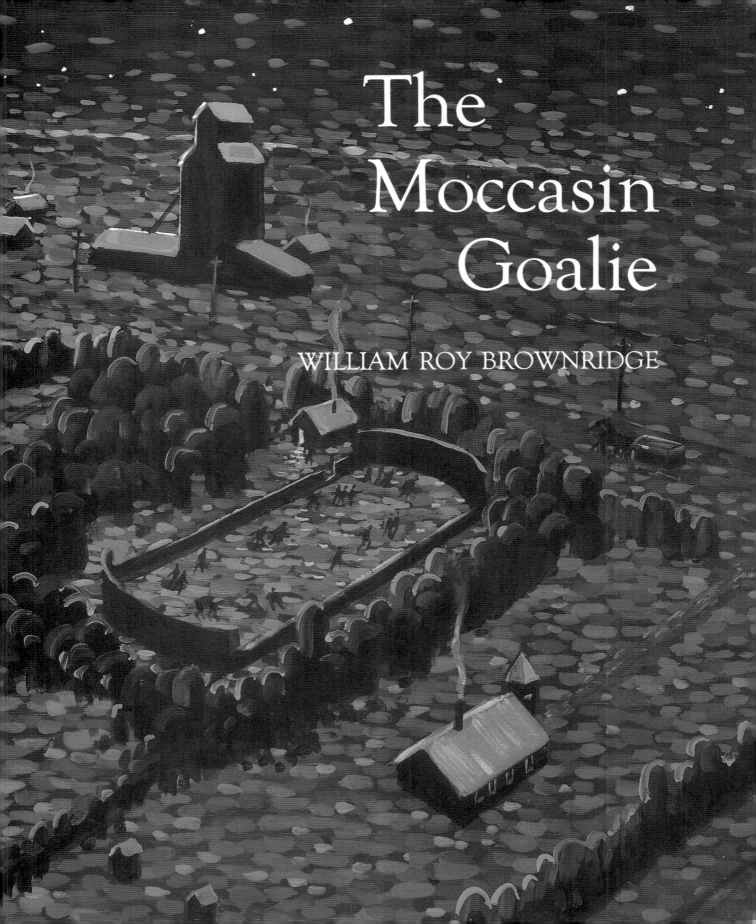

The
Moccasin
Goalie

WILLIAM ROY BROWNRIDGE

A long time ago when I was a boy, my family
lived on the prairies in a small town called
Willow. The winters there were very cold, with
the wind blowing the deep snow into huge drifts.
My friends and I didn't mind. This was our
favourite time of year. Cold temperatures meant
ice, and ice meant hockey!

I had four best friends. We lived for hockey.

Anita had long braids that flew out behind her when she skated. Marcel was big and quiet and good at sports. Then there was the tough little guy we nicknamed "Petou." And finally there was my dog Bingo, who always tried to steal the puck.

I was the goalie. I had a crippled leg and foot, so I couldn't wear skates. But my leather moccasins were just fine. I was quick and could slide across the goalmouth really fast. They called me "Moccasin Danny."

Before the really cold weather brought ice to our rink, we played road hockey right on Main Street in front of the Red & White store. Pieces of firewood or old overshoes marked our goals. We didn't have streetlights, and sometimes after dark we'd play by the light spilling from the store windows.

Often, on stormy days, Mom let us play inside with a soft ball of sponge rubber.

As time went by, we became more and more impatient for the day when we could play real hockey.

When winter finally arrived, the rink was the centre of attention. The men and big boys began the flooding. We watched as the ice became thick and smooth. Later, our job would be to keep it clear of snow. We spent hours scraping and sweeping so we could drop the puck on beautiful gleaming ice.

Dad said we had hockey on the brain. Mom said she heard me talking about hockey in my sleep.

One morning there was a surprise at the rink. Mr. Matteau gathered us together.

"We're going to have a hockey team. It'll be called the Wolves," he said. "I'll be your coach, and today I choose the team. What do you say, boys?"

We shouted and screamed with glee. This was going to be hockey heaven.

Everyone was silent as Mr. Matteau began reading out the names for the new team. Marcel was first to be called. The rest of us anxiously held our breath as other names were added. Finally Mr. Matteau put down his clipboard. Anita, Petou and I couldn't believe it. We were not on the team.

Marcel pointed to us and said, "They're good players."

Mr. Matteau shook his head. "Girls don't play hockey, Petou is too small and Danny can't skate."

When I got home, I told Mom what had happened.

"You and Petou and Anita can still have fun playing together," she said. "There will always be games of shinny at the rink."

This didn't make me feel any better. "It's not fair," I said. "We're just as good as the rest!"

Every night was the same. I lay awake staring at the ceiling and talking to myself. "My first chance to wear a uniform and play real hockey, and now it's gone."

Every day after school, I watched from my
window as the boys went to the rink. Bingo kept
looking at me and wagging his tail. He couldn't
understand why we didn't go out to play.
  Not making the team was the biggest
disappointment of my life.

Weeks later, one snowy Saturday, there was a
knock at the door. There stood Mr. Matteau,
pointing his finger at me and grinning.

"Danny," he said, "we need you to play goal this
afternoon. Tony is hurt. The league has given us
special permission to let you play on foot. This is
a very important game, you know. If we win,
we'll be in the play-offs."

I was so excited, I let out a whoop and jumped
back onto Bingo's tail. What a racket!

But even though I was happy, deep down I was
afraid. What if I let the team down?

When I got to the rink, all the guys patted me on the back and helped me into Tony's sweater. I was proud, but my heart was pounding.

Marcel whispered, "Don't worry. Just play your game and we'll win."

As I took my position in goal, I saw Anita, Petou and Bingo watching along the boards. "You can do it, Danny!" they called.

The first period was really rough, with end-to-end action. They scored on me and my spirits dropped, but then we scored twice. The period ended at two to one for the Wolves. I had stopped ten shots out of eleven. I could hardly breathe.

Then, in the second period, they attacked us with all their strength. I stopped twelve shots. But finally a shot went in over my pads. I felt sick. We were tied at two all. I'd let the team down.

The third period was like a bad dream. The shots came at me from all sides. I stopped them with every part of my body. It seemed impossible that we could win.

With only two minutes to go, Marcel rushed up the ice, stick handled through their defence and slipped the puck under their goalie. At the final whistle, we piled on top of each other in a great heap. We had won the game three to two!

Mr. Matteau came onto the ice and put his arms around Marcel and me. "You two saved the game for us," he said. "Danny, I want you to stay on the team. What do you say?"

I spotted Anita and Petou waving in the crowd. Suddenly I knew what I wanted most of all. I looked at Marcel and he nodded. I pointed to my friends and said, "They play the rest of the year with the Wolves, too."

Mr. Matteau laughed, but he promised. Then he took us all to Chong's Cafe for treats.

Our hearts glowed with the joy of victory. It was a night we would remember all our lives.

To Robert Roy "Bobby" Brownridge, who was my first
hero as a hockey player, pilot and brother, and
to my sisters, Gwendoline Brown and Kathleen Lake,
who advised and gave me support.
W.R.B.

Canadian Cataloguing in Publication Data
Brownridge, William Roy, 1932–
The moccasin goalie

ISBN 1-55143-054-1 (ppb)
I. Title.
PS8553.R798M62 1995   jC813'.54   C95-910448-8   PZ7.B76Mo 1995

The publisher would like to acknowledge the ongoing financial support of
The Canada Council, the Department of Canadian Heritage, and the
British Columbia Ministry of Small Business, Tourism and Culture.

Design by Christine Toller
Printed and bound in Hong Kong

Orca Book Publishers Ltd.
P.O. Box 5626, Station B
Victoria, BC Canada
V8R 6S4

Orca Book Publishers Ltd.
P.O. Box 468
Custer, WA   USA
98240-0468

10 9 8 7 6 5 4 3